Mockingbird

Mockingbird

ALLAN AHLBERG

ILLUSTRATED BY

PAUL HOWARD

CANDLEWICK PRESS
CAMBRIDGE, MASSACHUSETTS

Hush, little baby,
don't say a word,

Mama's gonna buy you . . .

a Mockingbird.

If that Mockingbird won't sing,

Papa's gonna buy you . . .

a garden swing.

If that garden swing gets stuck,
Polly's gonna buy you . . .

a pedal truck.

If that pedal truck tips over,

Rosie's gonna buy you . . .

a dog named Rover.

If that dog named Rover runs away,

Granny's gonna chase him . . .

if it takes all day!

If it takes all day and starts to . . .

rain,

Mama's gonna hurry you home again.

She'll wipe your face and dry your hair,

sit you up in your own highchair,

tie your bib and for goodness sake—

Papa's gone and baked you . . .

a birthday cake.

Tired little baby, Sleepyhead,
   Mama's gonna tuck you in your bed.
Close your eyes, don't say a word,

maybe have a dream . . .

of a Mockingbird.

For Collette and Kieran
— P. H.

Text copyright © 1998 by Allan Ahlberg

Illustrations copyright © 1998 by Paul Howard

All rights reserved.

First U.S. edition 1998

Library of Congress Cataloging-in-Publication Data

Ahlberg, Allan.

Mockingbird / Allan Ahlberg ; illustrated by Paul Howard. — 1st U.S. ed.

p.   cm.

Summary: A variation of an old lullaby in which adoring family
and friends promise the baby an assortment of presents.

ISBN 0-7636-0439-9

1. Folk songs, English — Texts. [1. Folk songs. 2. Lullabies.]

I. Howard, Paul, date, ill. II. Hush little baby. III. Title.

PZ8.3.A275Mo   1998

782.4215'82'0941 — dc21   [E]   97-18207

2 4 6 8 10 9 7 5 3 1

Printed in Belgium

This book was typeset in Usherwood Book.

The pictures were done in watercolor and crayon.

Candlewick Press

2067 Massachusetts Avenue

Cambridge, Massachusetts 02140